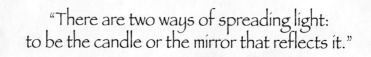

"There are two ways of spreading light:
to be the candle or the mirror that reflects it."

—Edith Wharton
THE VESALIUS IN ZANTE

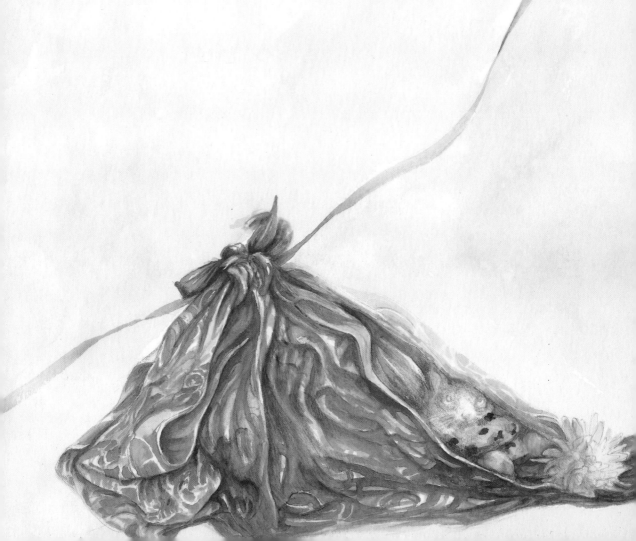

*For my sister, Irene, who makes me laugh,
and for my friend, June, who loves words.*
Phillipians 1:3 —R.T.

For Sarah Rose.
Jeremiah 29:11-13—D.S.

Published by
PEACHTREE PUBLISHERS, LTD.
494 Armour Circle NE
Atlanta, Georgia 30324

Text © 1996 by Ruth Tiller
Illustrations © 1996 by Debrah Santini

Jacket illustration by Debrah Santini

Printed in Hong Kong

10 9 8 7 6 5 4 3 2 1

First Edition

Library of Congress Cataloging-in-Publication Data
Tiller, Ruth.
    Wishing / by Ruth Tiller: illustrated by Debrah Santini. —1st ed.
       p. cm.
    Summary: Presents a lyrical expression of the power of the imagination
and the belief that wishes really do come true.
    ISBN 1-56145-118-5
    [1. Wishes—Fiction.] I. Santini, Debrah, ill. II. Title.
    PZ7.T458Wi 1996
    [E]—dc20   96-11720
                                CIP
                                AC

WISHING

By Ruth Tiller

Illustrated by Debrah Santini

PEACHTREE PUBLISHERS

ATLANTA

If I looked down and found
a wishing penny
winking from a weedy sidewalk crack,

I'd wish for you...

a day as bright as butter,
a red bandanna day,
with fat balloons bobbling on breezes
and pigeons sailing so high
they're specks of pepper in the sky.

If I strolled into a shady square that held
a wishing well
calmly waiting for my coin,

I'd wish for you...

a splash
of silver spray spewed aloft
by stone-carved dolphins
and burst of joyous song
from ruby-breasted robins
chorus-lined along a gabled roof.

If I turned through the park and chose
                        a drowsy dandelion
        nodding its fuzzy head in heavy sun,

                I'd wish for you...

a dappled pond where all the rocks

are smooth as watermelon seeds

and paper boats, like folded swans,

glide gracefully to tunes

of bullfrogs jamming in the reeds.

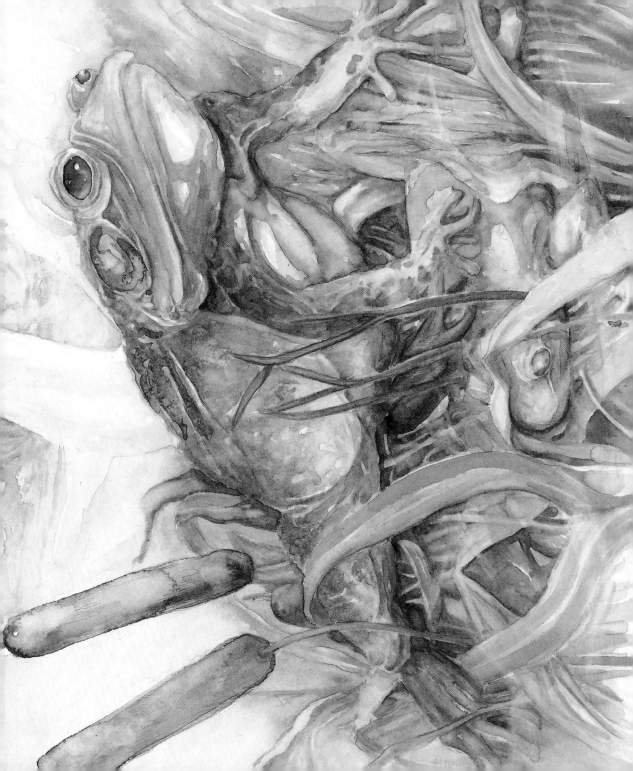

If I passed a rolling lawn and saw

   a pure white horse

      stretching its neck toward trailing clouds,

         I'd wish for you...

a field of rainbowed wild flowers,

a gentle hill to roll down,

an ancient arching cottonwood

with shimmered leaves that call,

"Come here, come climb."

If I should part my drapes and spy
the first star shine
within the blanketing of night,

I'd wish for you…

the coolest sip of water,
the softest drift of quilt,
a pocketful of secrets—
half a cookie, two blue marbles,
perhaps a white mouse-friend.

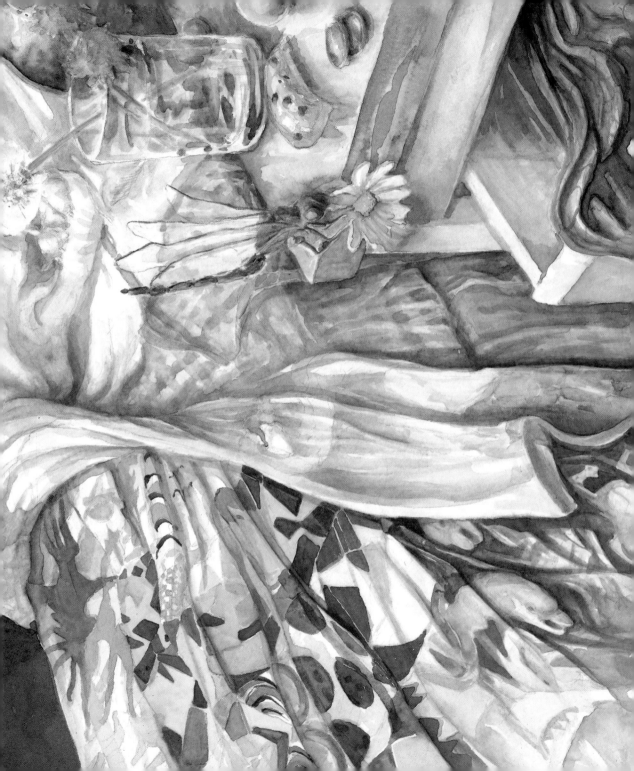

I'd wish you dreams
to tie in purple ribbons
and tuck beneath your pillow
until dawn.